D.W. SAVES the DAY

READ A BOOK WITH ARTHUR AND D.W.

• •

ARTHUR'S ADVENTURES

ARTHUR'S PET BUSINESS • ARTHUR'S BIRTHDAY • ARTHUR'S TEACHER TROUBLE

ARTHUR'S BABY • ARTHUR'S FIRST SLEEPOVER • ARTHUR'S CHRISTMAS

ARTHUR'S NEW PUPPY • ARTHUR BABY-SITS • ARTHUR'S CHICKEN POX

D.W.'S ADVENTURES

D.W. THE PICKY EATER • D.W. SAVES THE DAY

ARTHUR STICKER BOOKS

GLASSES FOR D.W. • ARTHUR'S READING RACE

ARTHUR CHUNKY LIFT-THE-FLAP BOARD BOOKS
ARTHUR GOES TO SCHOOL

D.W. SAVES the DAY

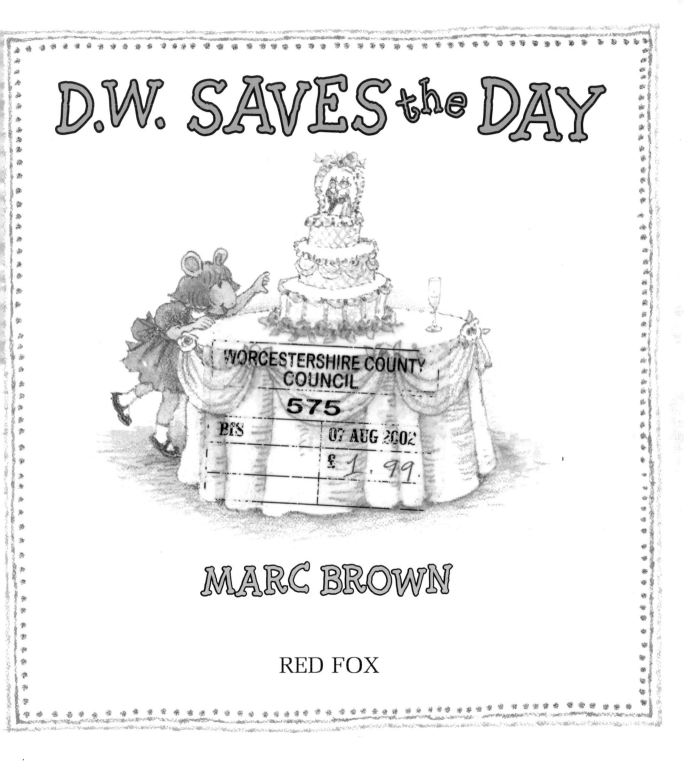

MARC BROWN

RED FOX

For Stacy, the bride,
Chris, the groom,
and Eliza, the flower girl

A Red Fox Book

Published by Random House Children's Books
20 Vauxhall Bridge Road, London SW1V 2SA

A division of Random House UK Ltd
London Melbourne Sydney Auckland
Johannesburg and agencies throughout the world

Copyright © 1993 Marc Brown

1 3 5 7 9 10 8 6 4 2

First published in the United States of America by Little, Brown
& Company and simultaneously in Canada by Little, Brown & Company
(Canada) Ltd 1993

First published in Great Britain by Red Fox 1998

Printed in Hong Kong

RANDOM HOUSE UK Limited Reg. No. 954009

ISBN 0 09 926316 5

Aunt Lucy was getting married in two hours.

Everyone was getting ready.

Arthur's job was to carry the wedding ring down the aisle.

He practised with his mother's ring.

"Why can't I be in the wedding, too?" asked D.W.

"Why can't I carry the ring?"

"You're too little," said Arthur. "And, besides, the ring bearer is always a boy. Everyone knows that."
"Be careful with my ring!" called Mother.
"At least I'd be able to keep the ring on the pillow!" said D.W.

"Let's get a picture of Arthur in his new suit," said Father.
"Straighten his tie, first," said Mother. "And put on your dress,
D.W., or we'll be late."

"Why can't I be bridesmaid?" asked D.W.
"I can walk slowly. I know how to hold my dress out
and take tiny steps."

"Cousin Cora is going to be bridesmaid,"
said Mother.
"She's older," said Father.
"She's my age," said Arthur.

"Why does Arthur get to sit in the front seat?" asked D.W.
on the way to the wedding.

"I have a very important job," said Arthur. "They can't get
married without the ring."

"That's true," said Father. "But try not to be nervous."

"Maybe Cousin Cora will get nervous, too," said D.W.

"Then I can be bridesmaid."

But Cousin Cora wasn't nervous at all.
And she was wearing pink nail polish. And shoes with bows.
"Look at my new dress!" said Cora. "It's great for swirling."
"I have a new bag," said D.W.
"With real pennies inside."

But Cora wasn't listening.
She was too busy twirling and swirling.
"I'm so excited!" said Cora.

D.W. went to find Aunt Lucy. She was very busy.
"Next time you get married, can I help?" asked D.W.
But with everyone talking, Aunt Lucy couldn't hear D.W.

Finally D.W. just sat down and watched everyone else get ready.

"Are you lost, little girl?" asked the photographer.

"I'm not little and I'm not lost!" said D.W.

"Hurry up, D.W.," said Mother.
"The wedding is about to begin."
"Good luck, Arthur," said Father.
"Don't forget to smile," said Grandma Thora.

The music began.
Cora set off down the aisle, holding her dress out and taking tiny steps.
"Why is everyone crying?" asked D.W. "Are they sad?"
"No," said Mother. "They're crying because they're so happy."

Arthur walked down the aisle after Cora.
He remembered to smile.
But when he stopped to wave to D.W., the pillow wobbled . . .
and the ring fell!

Arthur tried to catch it, but the ring began to roll faster
and faster down the aisle . . .
right into a grill.

"Now everyone really has something to cry about!" said D.W.
"Relax," said Uncle Shelly. "I'll get it."
He opened up the grill and looked in.
"It's a long way down!" he grunted. "I can't quite reach it."
"Let me try," said Arthur.

In he went.

"Your new suit!" cried Mother.

"Help!" cried Arthur. "I'm stuck!"

After they had pulled Arthur out, Cora offered to try.

"I think we need someone smaller," said Uncle Shelly.

"I'm small enough," said D.W. "Hold my feet."
Down she went.
THUMP! CLANK! CLONK!

And up she came.
"I found it!" she cried.
Everyone cheered.

The music began again.
This time it was D.W. who walked down the aisle.
Slowly, taking very tiny steps and careful to hold her dress out, she carried the ring.
She only stopped to let the photographer take her picture.

Finally, she reached the bride and groom.
"Thanks, D.W.!" whispered Aunt Lucy. "We couldn't have
done it without you."
"I may be little," said D.W., "but sometimes I can be
a big help!"